Just Like a Baby

by Rebecca Bond

Little, Brown and Company

Boston   New York   London

First Edition

Library of Congress Cataloging-in-Publication Data

Bond, Rebecca
    Just like a baby / Rebecca Bond — 1st ed.
        p.   cm.
    Summary: All the members of a family help create a beautiful cradle in anticipation of the arrival of a new baby.
    ISBN 0-316-10416-7
    [1. Cradles — Fiction.   2. Family — Fiction.   3. Babies —Fiction.]
  I. Title.
  PZ7.B63686Cr   1998
  [E]—dc21   98-15410

10 9 8 7 6 5 4 3 2 1

NIL

Printed in Italy

The paintings for this book were done in acrylic. The text was set in Dante. The display type was hand-lettered by Sue Dennen.

For my mother, who always told me I could
R.B.

When the family found out they were going to have a baby, they were all very excited.

"But where will the baby sleep?" Father asked. "What we need is a cradle."

That night, Father started to build a cradle. Carefully he measured and he sawed and he hammered. While he planed the boards and sanded them smooth, Father thought about ships rocking gently at sea. He thought about birds rocking gently in their nests at the top of tall trees.

After many days and nights at work, Father finally finished building the cradle. He stood back to admire it. The cradle looked solid and sturdy. It looked so sturdy, Father climbed in.

There in the cradle,
   Father rocked gently back and forth
   He rested within the smooth, sanded wood
   And he slept just like a baby.

The next morning, Grandfather came to see the cradle. "What a fine piece of work!" he said. "But something is missing. It needs to be painted."

On the inside of the cradle, Grandfather painted red fish in a deep blue sea. He painted elephants and giraffes and zebras. He painted white birds flying across a gold sky. It took him many days, and while he painted, he thought about the land and all the animals that shared this home. Now there would be one more to share it with.

After he had painted in the last bird, Grandfather walked around the cradle several times. The cradle shone with rich colors and magnificent animals. It was so beautiful, Grandfather decided to climb in.

There in the cradle,
    Grandfather rocked gently back and forth
    He rested within the smooth, sanded wood
    He looked at the fish and animals and birds
    And he slept just like a baby.

Grandmother came to see the cradle. "This is a lovely cradle," she said, "but something is missing. It needs a quilt."

Day after day, Grandmother worked beside the cradle, sewing together her quilt. While she sewed the colored pieces of cloth together, she thought about her family. Grandmother made a square on the quilt for each person in her family. She made a square for the new baby.

It took weeks to finish the quilt, but when she did, Grandmother laid it in the cradle. And now it looked so comfortable and warm, Grandmother simply had to try it. She climbed in.

There in the cradle,
　　Grandmother rocked gently back and forth
　　She rested within the smooth, sanded wood
　　She looked at the fish and animals and birds
　　She snuggled under the warm quilt
　　And she slept just like a baby.

Brother came to see how the cradle was coming along. "What a cradle!" he said. "But something is missing. It needs a mobile. I will make one."

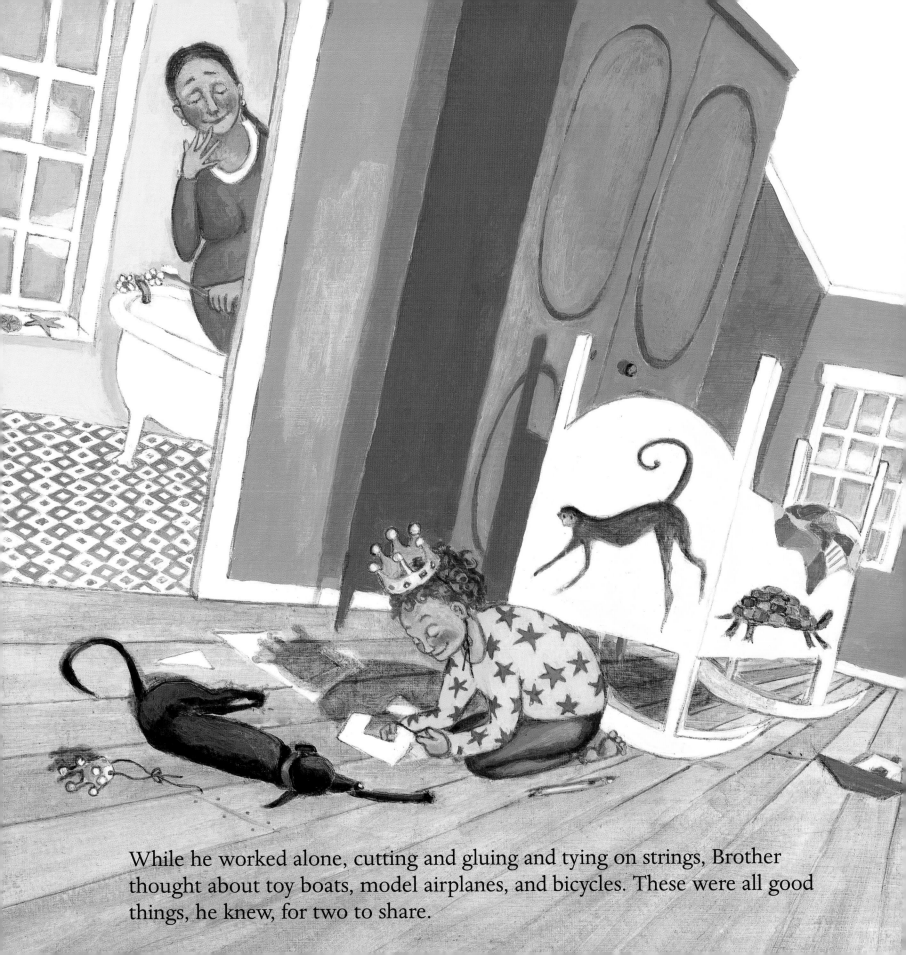

While he worked alone, cutting and gluing and tying on strings, Brother thought about toy boats, model airplanes, and bicycles. These were all good things, he knew, for two to share.

When Brother finished building his toy, he hung it over the cradle, and he looked at it. With the mobile turning above it, the cradle now looked fun to sleep in.

It looked so fun that Brother climbed in.

There in the cradle,
    Brother rocked gently back and forth
    He rested within the smooth, sanded wood
    He looked at the fish and animals and birds
    He snuggled under the warm quilt
    He watched the mobile slowly turn
    And he slept just like a baby.

Mother was getting very excited about the baby coming. She went into the room many times to look at the cradle. "This cradle is beautiful," she said, "but something is missing."

Slowly she pushed the cradle across the room to the windows. And as she positioned the cradle under the windows, she thought about the sky. She thought about the soft moonlight and the sweet morning sun. She thought about the stars and the cool night air.

Settled under the windows and glowing in pearly moonlight, the cradle was now finally complete. Mother felt it was ready for the baby. She smiled to herself.

There, next to the windows,
     Mother rocked the cradle gently back and forth
     She ran her fingers over the smooth, sanded wood
     She looked at the fish and animals and birds
     She turned down the warm quilt
     She watched the mobile slowly turn
     She saw the good sky shine softly through the windows
     And she felt the baby move inside her.

Finally, the baby arrived. One at a time, everyone in her family held her. They loved everything about her. They loved her round cheeks and her velvet skin. They loved her sweet milky smell. They loved the gurgles and warble sounds she made. She was warm and rosy and she fit easily into their arms. She was a very small person.

And then she started to cry. She wrinkled her tiny face and waved her tiny fists. She cried great loud cries. Her family watched in wonder. "What should we do?" they asked.

The family took her to her room. Carefully, they laid her down.
The crying stopped.

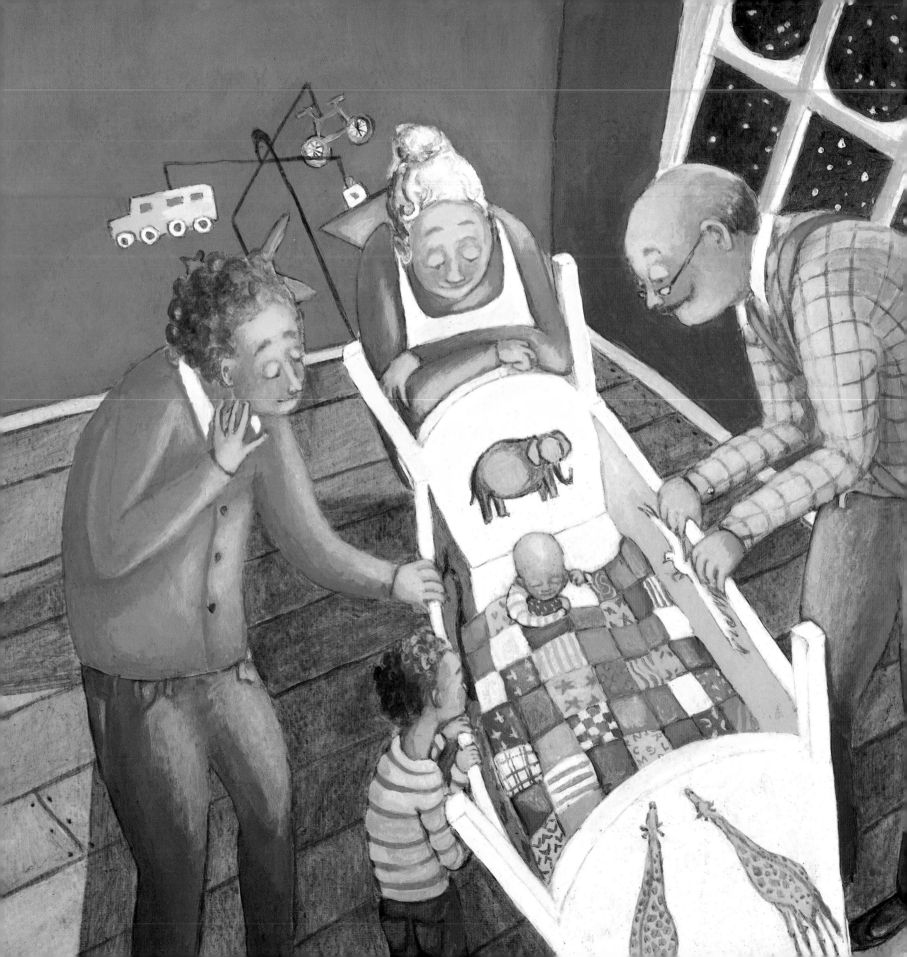

There in the cradle,
The tiny baby rocked gently back and forth
She rested within the smooth, sanded wood
She looked at the fish and animals and birds
She snuggled under the warm quilt
She watched the mobile slowly turn
She felt the good sky shine softly through the windows
She saw her family circled around her

And she slept just like a baby.